THE FOUR GETSYS
and What They Forgot

An I AM READING Book

By Annabelle Prager
Pictures by Whitney Darrow, Jr.

Pantheon Books

Library of Congress Cataloging in Publication Data
Prager, Annabelle. The four Getsys and what they forgot
(An I am reading book)
Summary: The Getsy family forgets everything, including where their shoes are.
[1. Shoes and boots—Fiction.   2. Memory—Fiction]
I. Darrow, Whitney, 1909-   II. Title.
PZ7.P8864Day 1982   [E]   81-5029
ISBN 0-394-84833-0   AACR2
ISBN 0-394-94833-5 (lib. bdg.)

To Jonathan
who has a very good memory

Chapter One

The Four Getsys were eating breakfast.
"What am I going to do?" said Betsy.
"It's almost time for school,
and my feet don't have
anything to wear."

"What's wrong with your shoes?"
said Mrs. Getsy.

"I forget what I did with them,"
said Betsy.

"They aren't anyplace."

"I can't find my shoes either,"
said Lenny Lew.

"Come to think of it," said Mr. Getsy,

"there weren't any shoes

in my closet this morning."

"This is terrible," said Mrs. Getsy.

"What are we going to wear

to the birthday party this afternoon?"

"Whose party is it?" asked Lenny Lew.

"I'd tell you if I could find
the invitation," said Mrs. Getsy.
"All I remember is
that we have to be there
at five o'clock on the dot."

"I know what I'll wear," said Betsy.

"My purple party dress and

my purple party shoes

with the criss-cross straps.

Oops, I almost forgot.

My party shoes are just as lost

as all the others."

"We can't go to a party

if we don't have shoes,"

said Mrs. Getsy.

"Everybody start looking right away."

Chapter Two

"Where do shoes go when they get lost?"

asked Mr. Getsy.

"Some shoes get kicked

under the sofa," said Lenny Lew.

"I'll see what I can find under there.

I don't see any shoes," he called,

"but there are a million other things.

What are these funny furry things?"

He held up two funny furry things.

"Those are my bunny slippers,"

said Betsy.

"I forgot that I had them."

"Was there a beautiful buttcrfly kite under the sofa?" asked Mr. Getsy.

"I let Betsy play with it yesterday and I haven't seen it since."

"There's a beautiful butterfly kite stuck at the top of the apple tree next door," said Lenny Lew.

"The next person who plays with my kite has to leave it where I can reach it," said Mr. Getsy.

"Oh dear, it's time to go," said Betsy, "and we still haven't found any shoes."

"Maybe the children lent their shoes to somebody at school," said Mrs. Getsy as she kissed the three Getsys goodbye.

Chapter Three

When Betsy got to school

Winkie Wolf shouted,

"Look at Betsy's feet!

They've got ears.

How come she's wearing
bunny slippers to school?"
"Maybe she's wearing bunny slippers
because the class is going to talk
about rabbits today,"
said the teacher, Miss Binks.

"Oh no, Miss Binks," said Betsy.

"I'm wearing them because

I don't have anything else to wear.

My whole family has lost their shoes.

Do you know where shoes go

when they get lost?"

"Some shoes go to the Lost and Found,"

said Miss Binks.

"You should go there too."

Betsy went straight to

the Lost and Found.

Lenny Lew was already there.

He had a bandage on his big toe.

"I got a splinter and it hurts,"

said Lenny Lew.

"Our shoes had better be here."

There were interesting things

in the Lost and Found.

Lenny Lew found

his Snoopy lunchbox

full of rotten forgotten lunch.

Betsy found the bottoms
of her pink pajamas.
But there weren't any shoes
in the Lost and Found,
not even one.

Chapter Four

While the children were at school

Mrs. Getsy looked for shoes.

She looked outside

and in.

She was looking in thc washing machine
when the phone rang.

"Is Betsy there?" said a little voice.

"She's not home yet," said Mrs. Getsy.

"Tell her to call her friend,

Joanie Jones.

It's very important,"

said the little voice.

"I won't forget," said Mrs. Gctsy.

She hung up the phone.

Just then Betsy and Lenny Lew
came home.

"Call your friend right away,"
Mrs. Getsy said to Betsy.
Betsy picked up the phone.
"You forgot to tell me
which friend to call," said Betsy.
"Her name slid right out of my mind,"
said Mrs. Getsy.

"And I'm too worried
about our shoes
to think of it right now."
"Where do shoes go
when they're not at home
and they're not at school?"
said Lenny Lew.
"Some shoes go to the shoemaker,"
said Betsy.
"That must be where our shoes are,"
said Mrs. Getsy.
"Let's go downtown and pick them up,"
said Lenny Lew.
"Hurry, hurry," said Mrs. Getsy,
"or you won't get them home
in time to wear them to the party."

Chapter Five

So Betsy and Lenny Lew
rode their bikes downtown
to the shoemaker.

"Do you have our shoes?"

Betsy asked the shoemaker.

"Of course I have your shoes,"
said the shoemaker.
"I wondered if you were ever
going to pick them up."
Betsy and Lenny Lew
jumped up and down with excitement
while the shoemaker went
to get their shoes.

"Here they are," said the shoemaker

holding up a tiny pair of shoes.

"Are these the only ones you have?"

asked Betsy.

"I didn't know I had such

teeny weeny feet."

"You don't have such teeny weeny feet

any more," said the shoemaker.

"These shoes were left here so long ago,

your feet have grown

four whole sizes since then."

"What are we going to do?" said Betsy.

"Our shoes aren't ANYPLACE."

"All shoes are someplace,"

said Lenny Lew.

"I have a great idea.

I know a place with a million shoes.

Maybe they have some they don't need."

Sure enough, down the street

was a store full of shoes.

Betsy saw a pair of purple party shoes

with criss-cross straps

just like the ones she used to have.

"May I borrow these for a little while?"
Betsy asked the man.

"We don't lend shoes," said the man.

"We sell them."

"But all my money is in the toe
of my old brown shoe," said Betsy.

"And my old brown shoe is gone."

A big tear ran down her cheek
as they walked out of the shoe store.

"I'm sick of wearing
funny bunny slippers," said Betsy
as they started walking home.
"Maybe we should forget
about going to the party."

33

Chapter Six

When Betsy and Lenny Lew got home
the phone was ringing.
Lenny Lew rushed to answer it.
"It's Joanie Jones from next door,"
shouted Lenny Lew.

"She says Betsy forgot to call her."

"Oh my," said Betsy.

"How could I forget to call Joanie?"

She picked up the phone.

"Hi Joanie," said Betsy.

"Say, Betsy," said Joanie, "did you know
that the beautiful butterfly kite
you were flying yesterday
is stuck at the top of our apple tree?"

"Oh dear," said Betsy.

"I hope you don't mind."

"It looks nice there," said Joanie.

"But the shoes look funny."

"What shoes?" said Betsy.

"All those shoes under the apple tree,"
said Joanie.

"And the ones that are stuck
in the branches.

My mother wanted to make an apple pie.

Now she says it will have to be
a shoe pie."

Chapter Seven

Everyone rushed next door

into Joanie's backyard.

Just as Joanie had said,

the ground under the apple tree

was covered with shoes—

big shoes, little shoes,

brown, red and blue shoes.

And hanging high in the branches

by their criss-cross straps

were two purple party shoes.

"Now I remember!" said Betsy

clapping her hands.

"There are the shoes

right where I threw them

out the window

at the apple tree."

"Why did you throw the shoes

out the window

at the apple tree?"

everybody asked all together.

"I didn't throw them

at the apple tree," said Betsy.

"I threw them

at Dad's beautiful butterfly kite

stuck at the top of the apple tree.

We have to get that kite down.

What can we throw now?"

"There's no time to throw

anything now," said Joanie.

"It's my birthday.

Did you forget?

I'm having a birthday party.

You have to be at my house

at five o'clock on the dot."

"Why should we forget?" said Betsy.

"We don't forget *everything*.

In fact I can't remember

one

    single

        thing

that we forgot today."

"Of course you can't," said Joanie.

"If you could you wouldn't be

one of the forgetful four Getsys."

Annabelle Prager was born in New York City and graduated from Sweet Briar College. She then studied at the Yale School of Fine Arts and the Art Students League, and was an illustrator for many years before she wrote her first two books for children, THE SURPRISE PARTY and its sequel, THE SPOOKY HALLOWEEN PARTY. She lives in Manhattan with her husband and their two children, Jonathan and Lucy.

Whitney Darrow, Jr. was born in Princeton, New Jersey. He graduated from Princeton University where he studied history and drew cartoons for the *Princeton Tiger.* He later attended the Art Students League and began drawing for magazines and advertisements. He has illustrated many books for children and is very well known for his *New Yorker* cartoons. He and his wife have two grown children and live in Connecticut.